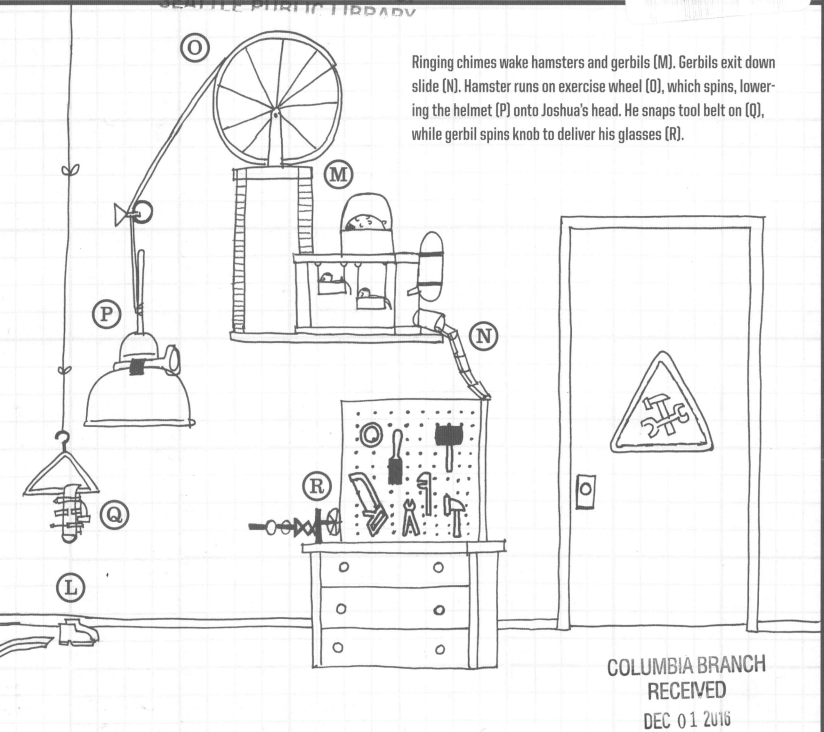

Ringing chimes wake hamsters and gerbils (M). Gerbils exit down slide (N). Hamster runs on exercise wheel (O), which spins, lowering the helmet (P) onto Joshua's head. He snaps tool belt on (Q), while gerbil spins knob to deliver his glasses (R).

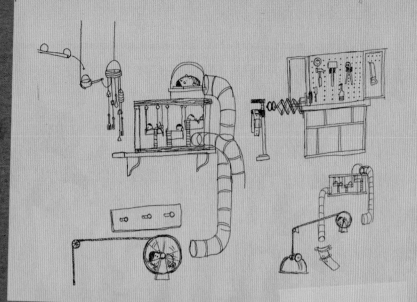

For Paul, my favorite
fix-it man, with love!
-S.H.

For Paul Stokstad,
thank you for being an uncle,
mentor, and friend.
-A.C.

Fix-it!

The Fix-It Man

Text copyright © 2016 by Susan Hood

Illustrations copyright © 2016 by Arree Chung

All rights reserved. Manufactured in China.

No part of this book may be used or reproduced in any manner whatsoever without
written permission except in the case of brief quotations embodied in critical articles and reviews.
For information address HarperCollins Children's Books, a division of
HarperCollins Publishers, 195 Broadway, New York, NY 10007.

www.harpercollinschildrens.com

ISBN 978-0-06-237085-3 (trade bdg.)

The artist used paper collage, duct tape, string, watercolors, ink, and
Photoshop to create the illustrations for this book.

16 17 18 19 20 SCP 10 9 8 7 6 5 4 3 2 1

❖

First Edition

THE Fix-It MAN

Words by Susan Hood
Pictures by Arree Chung

HARPER
An Imprint of HarperCollinsPublishers

YAWN.

Joshua James is the Fix-It Man.
If he can't fix it, no one can!

He snaps his tool belt,
dons his hat.

SNAP!

He swings his hammer—

RAT-A-TAT-TAT!

He pounds a peg

and turns a screw,

but that's not all that he can do.

When things conk out or crash or crack, he tinkers till they're back on track. Fix a flat?

Repair a wreck?

Build a bridge?

CHECK
CHECK
AND
CHECK!

With Joshua James, it won't take long
to look around and fix what's wrong.

P.U. Those diapers sure do stink.
Clipboard out! It's time to think!

No job's too big,
beyond repair,

but some require extra care.

If one solution just won't do,

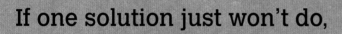

the Fix-It Man
can try Fix Two.

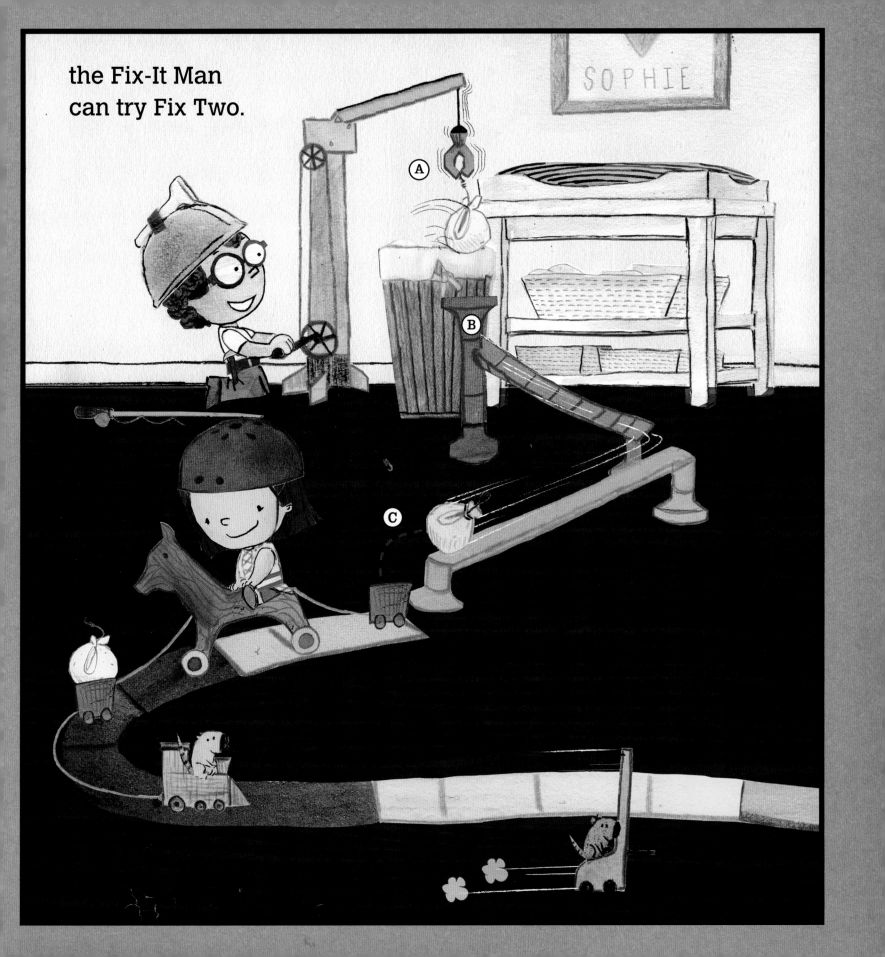

At times like these, you may have heard,
the best fix is a single word!

Success! The system is a go.
Here they come! Look out below!

Let's hear it for the Fix-It Man.
That stinky problem's in the can!

Well, almost. . . .

Everyone goofs, and things can break.
Even dads can make mistakes!

A helping hand, a hug or two
will fix him up as good as new.

One never knows just how or why
new problems tumble from the sky.

No fix-it tricks can mend this crack.
The deed is done—no going back!
So if a fix leaves you perplexed,
wait and see . . .

what happens next!

Things may need to break in two
to bring the world something new!

OPERATION: DUMP THE DIAPERS

Toy crane lifts diaper from diaper pail (A) and drops on ramp (B), where it slides down to train car (C). Train carries diaper to gerbil's forklift (D). He lifts it to Ferris wheel car (E). Diaper rides up belt (F) and is hooked by paper clip (G). It travels until scissors clip it (H) and it falls to ramp (I) below.

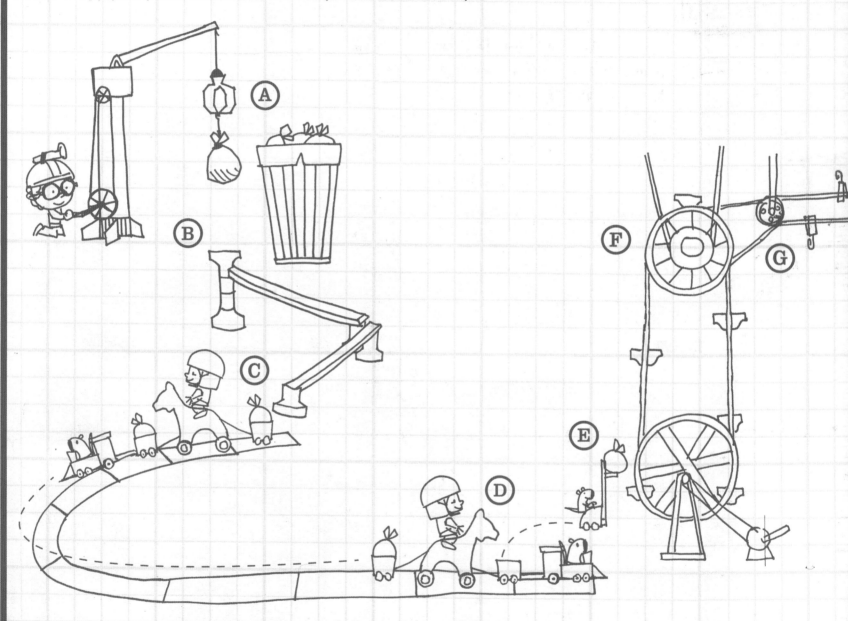